I0176750

Pull Your Pants Up

AND BE A MAN!

Bernice Harris

Contribution from Stefanie Newell
Foreword by Malik Yoba

Write One Publications, Inc.

Marietta, GA

Copyright © 2009 by Bernice Harris.

All rights reserved. No part of this publication may be repro-
duced, distributed or transmitted in any form or by any means,
including photocopying, recording, or other electronic or me-
chanical methods, without the prior written permission of the
publisher, except in the case of brief quotations embodied in
critical reviews and certain other noncommercial uses permit-
ted by copyright law. For permission requests, write to the
publisher, addressed "Attention: Permissions Coordinator," at
the address below.

Write One Publications, Inc.
PO Box 454
Smyrna, GA 30081

www.howtowriteabookthatsells.com

Pull Your Pants Up/Bernice Harris. — 2nd ed.

ISBN 978-0-9821484-6-4

Contents

Dedication

This book is dedicated to every boy who reads it and who understands that change is possible, and who will not hesitate to do what it takes to make those changes. A big "thank you" to my family and friends who have given me so much support for this project. To my husband, John, who is always kind and patient, and who gave me that extra boost to keep writing. Thanks to my friend Viola Scott (Mikki), whose friendship and encouragement have been there for me over the years, including during this endeavor. I must not forget my mentor, Rosie Wells, of Rosie Wells Enterprise, who believed in me, years ago. She encouraged me and demonstrated her trust in my writing abilities by placing me on her staff of writers in the Collectors Bulletin magazine. And last but not least, Write One Publications, Inc., who swayed from their preferred genre and published this book because they felt it was important and needed.

What Others Are Saying...

Pull Your Pants Up and Be A Man! is a timely book that is definitely needed to encourage African American males to reach their full potential. The practical wisdom provided on a variety of essential topics speaks directly to the hearts of African American males. Every African American male and those who are concerned about his well-being should have this book on their shelves. This book is destined to be a classic!!

Chance W. Lewis, Ph.D.

Endowed Chair and Associate Professor of Urban Education, Texas A&M University

As a mentor to men in the village of Harlem and abroad, I highly recommend Pull Your Pants Up and Be A Man! This teaching tool will enhance your ability to address sensitive issues that are crippling our community. This book will certainly set a standard that will cause others to strive for success and seize it!

Dr. Kris F. Erskine, Sr. Pastor
Bethany Baptist Church-Harlem

BY MALIK YOBA

Foreword

WHAT MADE YOU PICK UP this book? Was it a parent? A teacher? A friend? Was there simply a little voice inside that said "Hmmm....who do these people think they are having the nerve to tell me to pull my pants up and be a man?! They don't know me!" I don't know about you, but when I first heard about this book and the title, that was the first thought that I had. And then I thought, let me look further into this and see what they have to say about being a man. I thought that anybody who cares enough to take the time to write a book about one of the hardest jobs a guy will ever have — being a man, I wanted to at least take the time to read up on it. What I found was very thought provoking.

The questions asked in this book are the same questions I asked of myself as a young person, and they are the questions I ask my son and daughters to consider.

Who are you? Why are you on this planet? What does it mean to be responsible, accountable and live with integrity? How do you plan and work towards fulfilling all of those dreams floating around in your head? I feel very fortunate to have had my own father as a living example of so many positive traits of manhood. He was hardworking in his traditional job as an x-ray technician in a hospital but he was also an entrepreneur and always told us "Build your own generator, so when they turn off the power, you still have lights!"

He was big on looking out for our neighbors, literally. He assisted many families around us with food, money and shelter. He taught us that our "word" was the most important thing we can give somebody and not to make promises that we couldn't keep. He taught us the value of looking someone in the eyes and having a strong grip during a handshake, and how important that was in order for people to take us seriously...this applied to my sisters as well.

But most importantly, he taught my siblings and me how to think critically, to never downplay our intelligence and to strive for excellence in everything we do.

I understand that there are many young men and boys that look like me that don't have their fathers in the picture. They have no concept of what it means to be a man other than from watching TV and movies! For many young men that look like me, they believe it's all about money, cars, jewels and women! Of course, there is nothing wrong with those things but if they are not tied to a critical way of thinking about ourselves from the inside out, those material possessions alone will never fully satisfy us whether we know it or not. We have to get our minds right. We have to be careful and really consider what we think about. We have to watch the kinds of thoughts we focus on. We have to gain greater access to our spiritual essence, our intuition, deep levels of compassion and an understanding of being absolutely responsible for the causes and effects of our actions.

This book that you are holding in your hands is designed to be one piece of the lifelong process/puzzle called *Pull Your Pants Up* "self improvement." So congratulations! Improving yourself is a wonderful and worthy endeavor! It is the first step to creating the life YOU SHOULD WANT; one of abundance, happiness, good health, a loving family, a great career and community service. This life is about watching what you think and controlling your thoughts. It will lead you to believe that there is no limit to your greatness and purpose, and that only fear and ego can keep you from

God's promise for your life. You did not create the physical body that you are in or the family that you were born into. However, you can control your mind. Ask yourself, "In the course of my average day, are my thoughts mostly negative or positive? Do I believe that I can achieve anything my heart desires or do I feel limited by my current circumstance?" Tiger Woods, Lebron James, Jay-Z and former President Barack Obama, like all successful people have one thing in common — they all believed the success they achieved to date was possible the minute the idea was formed in their head. The same is possible for you.

If you dream of doing great things with your life, but those around you do not feel the same way, you must watch how you begin to think as a result of that. We cannot afford to let doubt, fear and confusion take over. We must all keep a firm grip on the true desires of our hearts. I tell my kids all the time that they are not allowed to use the phrase "I can't." They are encouraged on a regular basis to think "outside the box" and to dream as big as possible without ever putting a limit on themselves. That's what this book is all about. It is designed to help you dream, plan and execute the necessary steps that it takes to becoming that refined, classy, successful gentleman that you always dreamt you would become. Enjoy!

Malik Yoba

P.S. I would love to hear from you.

Follow me on: Twitter.com/malikyoba or
Email me at info@pleasereturnmyphonecall.com.

CHAPTER 1

Goals

Minds are like parachutes, they only function when they are opened. — Sir James Dewar

HEY YOUNG MAN; YES, YOU! What kind of plans are you making for your life? Have you given serious thought to the future? Are you taking an active role in making things happen for yourself? Are you sitting back, waiting to see what happens in your life, without putting serious effort into mapping out the life that you want for yourself? Are you taking the attitude "whatever will be, will be?" Are you now leading a life that will assure you of doing all that you are capable of doing?

Think of people you know, whom you consider successful, with good careers and happy families. How did they acquire that? That person who never did much with his or her life and is constantly unhappy or in trouble —

how did he get there? If this has not been important to you in the past, or if you have not given much thought to people in that way, please take a little time to do so. See if you can single out the life planners from the ones who did not do very much in steering their lives in a positive direction. What you will discover about people will be an eye-opener!

After you have reflected on your friends and acquaintances, focus on a few people who are well known by the world. Here are a few excellent examples of successful life planners to get you started:

Tiger Woods was born in 1975. From an early age, he was groomed by his father to be a success. At the age of two years old, he was putting with Bob Hope, a seasoned golfer, on *The Mike Douglas Show*. Tiger turned professional in 1996, and in the same year, he was named Sportsman of the Year by *Sports Illustrated Magazine*. He was the most successful athlete in 2005 and one of the highest-paid athletes in 2006, earning a whopping $87 million. Did his success just happen or was it planned?

Another good example of a person with goals is the singer Usher. At the age of fifteen, he released his first CD. Had Usher never recognized that he had a talent and the ability to perform and entertain audiences, and was satisfied with merely singing along to the radio or to another singer's music, what would he be doing today? If he didn't have a vision of what he wanted to do with his life, would his friends and family have been the only recipients of his talents? If hanging out with his buddies, who had no real interest in his dream, became more important than what he loved to do, how do you think his life would have turned out?

Michael Jordan was one of the most accomplished basketball players of all time. Suppose he was satisfied with just being a spectator, without ever participating in the game of basketball. If he had not practiced shooting baskets and jumping higher than anyone else, with the goal of becoming the best at his sport, he could be the man sitting next to you at the basketball game, watching other goal-setters play out their dreams. The number 23 may have been on the jersey of another basketball player. Joseph Smith, Brian Johnson, Kevin Hill, and Darrell Green are fictional names of players who may have been wearers of that famous number.

These men were not afraid to make goals, and they worked toward carrying them out. These three achievers are just a small sample of young men who did not leave their future to chance. They did not wake up one day and have things start happening for them without preparation and effort on their parts.

Each of these men—Tiger Woods, Usher, and Michael Jordan—is a mega moneymaker. However, if you asked any of them about their life's achievements and what they were most proud of, their monetary earnings would probably not be what they would say brought them the most satisfaction. The setting of goals and the accomplishment of those goals would top each of their lists.

Now that we have talked about famous people and their achievements, return your focus to your close friends. Have you heard them speak of their goals lately, about what they would like to be doing five, ten, or twenty years from now? What about you? Have you thought that far ahead? Until now, have your plans been on hold because you felt that other things were more important? You do not want to spend more time planning the kind of gym shoes that you want to buy instead of something as important as your future.

If you were traveling from Chicago to New Orleans and you had never made the trip before, right away your first questions might be, "How far is it?" "How many states will I cross before I arrive at my destination?" "How far will I travel before I will need food and gas?" "Is the trip so long that I will need to spend the night somewhere?" "What will the road conditions and weather be like during my travel?" "Will my car need to be serviced in order to make a trouble-free trip?" "Which interstate highway will I travel?" "Should I take the shorter route or the more scenic one?"

To prevent aimlessly wandering off on the wrong route—after giving so much attention to all of the other details of the trip—a clear, detailed map is a must. If such careful planning is required for a trip that will take hours, much more planning is needed to plan a life that could span over sixty or seventy more years. In a world where technology is advancing at such a rapid pace, it is impossible to imagine what the next few years will bring as far as new inventions. The cell phones, game consoles, computers, and high-definition televisions of today will be replaced by technology that is more sophisticated and innovative. Prepare now so you will have enough money to be a consumer of those goods.

For you, planning for the future may mean getting serious about school now, taking advantage of every opportunity to learn and excel in your studies. If you have left school or are thinking about leaving, reconsider. You can still be a success. However, you must buckle down, make a firm commitment, and start to make goals for yourself.

Small children are asked the question from the time that they are four or five years old: "What do you want to be when you grow up?" Without pausing, the child will spurt out two or three unrelated occupations without pausing for a breath. "I want to be a fireman, a doctor, and I want to drive a train, too." They may even think that they can work at all of these jobs simultaneously.

The inquirer will then engage the child in conversation on their fantasy future occupations without putting a seed of doubt in the mind of the dreamer. Neither will the parents put anything negative into their child's mind to make him think that those goals are impractical.

As the child gets older, he or she may be asked the same question by another person. The inquirer at this point will probably whittle away at some or most of the child's goals by telling the child that it is impossible to do all of those jobs. "You will have to choose one," they might say.

Later, someone else may comment upon the child's lack of ability to do either of his future dream jobs. Soon, what started out as confidence will give way to self-doubt, and then giving up altogether.

Those future occupations will soon be forgotten and the young person will go into life accomplishing far less than he was probably capable of if a well-meaning person—who was only trying to make conversation with a young child—had not planted the negative thoughts.

What were some of your goals when you were a child?

_____

_____

_____

_____

_____

_____

_____

Are those still your goals? Why or why not?

List two people who can help you to reach your goals.

_____

_____

_____

_____

_____

_____

_____

_____

Bernice Harris

CHAPTER 2

Dreams

No lower can a man descend than to interpret his dreams into gold and silver. —Kahil Gibran

YOU PROBABLY HAD DREAMS and the confidence that you could do anything that you desired, with no thought at all of obstacles or failure. What happened to your dream? When did you stop dreaming? Who stole your dream? Listen to this story and see if it can help you to dream again.

Once there was an old man who had knowledge and wisdom about everything. He knew the answer to any question that was asked of him or any problem that was presented to him. If someone had a question about love, he knew the answer. If he was asked a question about getting along with others, he knew the answer to that, too. Questions about science would get an immediate correct response.

One day, a young man wanted to outsmart the old man. So he caught a bird and brought it to the old man. After carefully placing the bird into the palms of his hands and hiding it behind his back, he asked the wise old man a question. "Old man, is the bird alive or is it dead?" If the old man said "alive," he would squeeze the bird to death. If the old man said "dead," he would open his hand and let the bird fly away. The wise old man was aware that he was being tricked, so he looked straight into the eyes of the young man and said, "Young man, it is in your hands; it can be whatever you want it to be."

The answer that was given to the young man can also apply to you. "Your future is in your hands; it can be whatever you want it to be." Does your life plan have to follow the path of others that you admire? Should you try to imitate the choices others have made?

No. Your values, talents, and experiences make you different from all others. Use your uniqueness to carve out your own place in the world. You can be just as successful doing what you are good at doing and what you love to do, as those who you may want to imitate. Keep in mind that success is not having a glitzy lifestyle, making millions and millions of dollars. Success can also be making a moderate salary and using much of your time volunteering to help others. Living a life of giving and helping—without focusing all of the emphasis on what you want to acquire for yourself—can be a very fulfilling life.

You do not want to waste precious time trying to pursue a career that requires a special talent, such as becoming a famous singer, if your talent is in another area. Doing so would only lead to frustration. However, you can imitate the setting of goals and the ambition that singers, actors, and others put into their life's work. Here, another caution is in order. It would be a misuse of your time to imitate the lifestyles that you see in the movies, on television, or at awards shows. You are not seeing the real person, but rather the public image that is needed for their work. In real life, they are just ordinary people with the same worries, insecurities, and sorrows as anyone else. Trying to imitate them would be like trying to become someone that even the person you are trying to imitate is not. Remember, no one can be a better *you* than *you*. You are unique! Knowing this, you can now find and work on the real you. It will take self-examination along with a small amount of help from the outside.

Let's look at a few areas of your life where — if you give it close attention — you will get surprising results. So pull your pants up and be a man as you set off on the quest to find the real and better YOU.

Begin thinking about your dream. What have you dreamed for your life after high school?

_____

_____

_____

_____

_____

_____

_____

_____

What person do you admire that followed their dream?

_____

_____

_____

_____

_____

_____

_____

_____

What aspects of their achievements would you like to pursue?

What will you need to learn in order to accomplish your dream?

_____

_____

_____

_____

_____

_____

_____

CHAPTER 3

Self-Esteem

Nothing builds self-esteem and self-confidence like accomplishment. — Thomas Carlyle

YOUR FIRST CONCERN IN FINDING the real you should start with a few questions. Who is the real me? When I sit alone with my thoughts, how do I feel about myself? Do I like the person that I am becoming? Am I hiding the real me because, if others knew that I had the desire to do something constructive with my life, I would be made fun of? Who am I without the street names given to me by my friends?

These questions are not asked without purpose, but to get you to think of the perception you have of yourself, and how you are viewed by others. What type of clothing do you wear? Did you know that some styles began within the walls of the prison system?

If the way that you are presenting yourself is not conforming to the real person that you are inside, are you willing to make adjustments to become your true self by matching the good person that you are inside with what you show to the world on the outside?

You probably have grouped people that you have met. Think of a young man with his pants two inches above his ankles. He has on a tight, faded t-shirt with "1999" written across the front. He is wearing black lace-up shoes, his glasses are thick rimmed, and he is sporting a very bad haircut. Maybe he is even reading a book. Can you put him into a group? Is he a nerd who does lots of reading? Is he a shy person that you would not like to spend much time with because he would be too boring? Would you find him hard to talk to because his interest would be extremely different from your own? Your view of the young man could be a complete misrepresentation of who he really is. If you talked with him for a short time, you might find that you have many of the same interests. Very little of what you previously thought about him may be true.

As a matter of fact, you may find that you share more interests than differences. You may also discover the person to be the complete opposite of what you thought.

Are you beginning to see how people can be mislabeled and put into a group based on their outward appearance, without ever speaking a word?

Maybe you have defined yourself by what has been said to you in a hurtful way and you are trying to disguise your inner feelings of hurt. You may wish that people would see a different person than what you feel inside. If this is true, then it is time to do a little inner searching. If you were asked right now about your abilities, what would you say? Are your having troubles with your reading and math, which have made it tough for you to keep up with others? Poor reading and math difficulties can be improved with time. Help and much study may be needed, and it does not have to overshadow your entire life.

Recall your early years and how you were made to feel about your abilities. Remember when you drew that picture of your house with all of the stick family peering out of the windows and with the bright orange sun shining over the rooftop? Do you remember how that drawing brought flattering compliments from your teacher? "Good job," she probably said. When you took your drawing home, nice things were said about your artistic abilities. Your mother hung your drawing on the refrigerator for everyone to admire and comment on. That made you feel proud. You knew that you were the best at what you were doing.

As you grew older, your basketball coach may have added to your self-esteem when you made that important shot that meant your team would either win or have a chance at winning. Was that not an awesome moment that showed you excelled at what you could do? Your dad may also have given you a big boost from the crowd when he yelled, "That's my boy!" All of those words and actions were positive and added to your self-esteem.

The opposite may also be true in your experience. You may have been raised in a home where you had an absent father or mother. You may not have been brought up by your natural mother and father. Instead of praise, you may have received constant criticism that lowered your self-esteem.

Later, some unimportant person may have said something to you or about you in passing that was unkind and not based on the truth. However, you took those words on as true, and that became the new way you felt about yourself. Hurtful words, no matter how innocent, can be life changing and can have a big enough impact to make life less than it could be.

That thoughtless person who made the negative remark about you may not know the effect his words had on your life. He has perhaps gone on to make a good life for himself—unless someone had said something to him as well that destroyed his own self-esteem.

A lady who is now an adult was teased by an acquaintance as a young girl. She was told that she had big feet. Those words were not true at all. The girl was quite petite with normal-sized feet. It did not matter what she saw when she looked at her feet, but rather what the adult told her about her feet. For a long time, she would hide her feet underneath her chair when he came around. Until this day, she still thinks of those cruel words spoken to her about her feet.

Since that time, many important things have happened in her life that have been forgotten. However, she still remembers the few negative words spoken about her feet.

Words carry much power. You should be very careful how you use words when speaking to others. You should also be careful of how you allow other's negative words to influence you.

Children were taught an old saying years ago to use when they were bullied or teased by others: "Sticks and stones may break my bones but words can never hurt me." Those words are partially true.

Sticks and stones can break bones but unkind words can also hurt deeper than can be imagined. But as bad and hurtful as words and other things that have taken place in your life may have been, you can still move ahead and make a good life for yourself. Millions of people from similar—or even worse—backgrounds than yours have gone on to accomplish many good things.

In your pursuit to find the real you, the knowledge that there is not another person exactly like you will help you to find your real place in the world. It can also mean an end of striving to imitate the public image of famous people, as you begin to understand your own uniqueness. You will then not have to define yourself by whether you have money or the lack thereof, or whether you are dressed in the latest fad that hides who you really are. Nor will you allow companions to push you into a course that you have not planned and do not desire to go. Real men lead and are not easily pushed.

That real person that you found in the quietness of your room is ready to come out. He needs to be worked on—get to it. The time is right for change!

Bernice Harris

My best traits are....

_____

_____

_____

_____

_____

_____

_____

_____

Pull Your Pants Up!

_____

_____

_____

_____

_____

_____

_____

_____

The traits that I need to work on are...

_____

_____

_____

_____

_____

_____

_____

_____

_____

_____

_____

_____

_____

_____

_____

_____

CHAPTER 4

Education

Do just once what others say you can't do, and you will never pay attention to your limitations again. —James R. Cook

IF THE RIVER IS SUCCESS, then education is the bridge that will get you across. Careful planning and preparation for the future starts with early and focused attention on your goals.

The years that you will work and support yourself and possibly a family may seem a long way off. However, years come quickly, and if good, sound decisions are not made early, it could be a cause for real regret. It will also have a great impact on how life will turn out for you in later years.

A few years ago, your parents started to teach you the alphabet. In the beginning, you may have only been able to recite "A...B...C" and count only to three. Your parents knew that, in time, you would learn all 26 letters and you would put them together to form short words like "sat," "cat," "boy," and "toy."

Later on, you would be able to make every possible word in the English language from those 26 letters. In addition, the most complex mathematical calculations could be solved using those first numbers that you learned: zero through ten. In time, you took an interest in writing your name and more of the numbers. Your handwriting may not have been very clear at first, but you were well on your way to a world of practicing and perfecting a skill that you would use for a lifetime.

Identifying colors and objects began in the home and was expanded upon when you entered pre-school and kindergarten. You learned your first social skills at home. These skills were reinforced in your early child-hood education in a more structured setting. Sharing, taking turns, and being aware of others' feelings and knowing how to express your own were some of the important things that you learned in your early education.

Since that time, just think of what you have learned passively, without any real effort on your part. Listening to the radio, watching television, traveling, and reading for pleasure helped you to learn numerous things. Listening to and participating in conversations allowed you to take in massive amounts of knowledge and you may not even have been aware that you were learning at the time.

All of this information certainly has been useful as you have progressed through life and arrived at this point. Not unlike what has already taken place with your learning, the above examples show that education is a continual process, one that starts early and continues throughout life.

Those first baby steps that you took in gaining knowledge will eventually become a giant leap that will land you where you want to be. Now, you need to concentrate on the years of your life where education is not obtained passively, but is rather a consciously planned process. Most of these planned years are spent in public or private schools, and many of the courses that you will study have been predetermined in order to give you the education that you will need for future employment and to make sure that you are a well-rounded person.

Some young men may decide during the last part of these structured learning years that some of it is not for them. For certain individuals, the decision may be to show little or no interest in what is being taught in the classroom. Socializing with friends and goofing off may become more important than learning. The more difficult subjects like science, algebra, history, and literature may seem too challenging to even consider. Teachers may become the archenemy that is out to get them. The classroom now becomes a battleground for the student's attention. The motivators that may have been in the young person's mind are no longer goals, but rather irritants.

Think back to the young years, and how a child can talk about what he or she wants to be when grown up, without a hint of doubt. If a large amount of that kind of enthusiasm has been lost in you, then serious efforts have to be made to retrieve it. Appreciation for the role of teachers can give you some insight into their part in helping you get your dream back. Teachers can help you develop into the man that you need to become.

Pretend that you are running a long-distance race. Along the way, you will need water to keep you hydrated in order to make it to the finish line. Several people have volunteered to hand out water at various points in your run. You are not interested in the personalities and other attributes of the volunteer who is giving you the water. Your encounter will be brief.

Whether the water-giver is kind, understanding, grouchy, or impatient is not important. Your main concern is what they have in their hand to help you win the race.

You can look at your school years in much the same way as the runner in the race. Teachers have a variety of personalities and different levels of dedication to their work. Some will be dull and uninteresting. Others will be good teachers who have burned out over the years from the lack of interest from students whose lives they had hoped to change. Their efforts were not crowned with complete success. Then there will be very interesting, creative teachers who will make learning a fun experience, rather than a dull or boring one. Regardless of the different types of teachers that you meet in your search for an education, they all have one thing in common. They are passing valuable information on to you that will aid you in becoming a productive person. Therefore, the person who gives you information at this point should matter very little. Just as the water-giver's personality is not important to the runner, the knowledge passers' (teachers') personality should not be your focus. Your encounters with them will be brief. Besides, just like the runner in the race, you want to win!

Most teachers, as you have probably discovered, do not come into your life to stay. They are there for a short time to impart something of value to you, whether you like or dislike them. Do not resolve to make the crucial decision to show little interest in school or decide that dropping out of school is the thing to do because of your feelings about a particular teacher.

Study hard and become a class participator. Ask questions and raise your hand when you know the answers. Do not be shy about asking for help when you do not understand. If you have not been doing this up until now, it will surely grab the attention of your teachers— but in a positive way.

Often, students who show interest in what is going on in the classroom may be teased by their classmates. If you do not feel strong enough at this point to face your classmates with a new attitude about learning, involve some of your friends. Make a deal with them to become good students by studying together. Set short- and long-term goals and stick to them. In no time at all, you will be at the place you need to be.

Students and teachers, along with their personalities, are a sample of the people that you will meet in your work and social contacts in the outside world. So learn as much as you can about people and how to get along with them. This will be very helpful in the future.

Every day, you probably face metal detectors, strict rules on what you can bring to school, and even rules on what you can wear. This can be very annoying, especially when you are coming of age and looking for more freedom. These rules and restrictions, however, are there to keep you safe and to make sure that you are in an environment that enables you and others to get the best education possible. Rules will not end when you leave your home or school, but will follow you throughout your life. Everyone is, and will always be, governed by some rules and restrictions. Some of these will be wearisome.

Other limits on your life will not make much difference at all. Society, as chaotic as it may seem sometimes, has a basis of rules and limitations. If you have left school and you have been away for a year or two, no amount of encouragement will get you back into a classroom where your former classmates are now one or two years ahead of you. This is especially true if they have graduated and moved on to college or into the working world. Thus, a few more questions should be asked at this point.

Have your parents given up on you because of your resistance to education? Do you no longer receive encouragement because you have lost faith to do anything positive or useful with your life? Are you where you are because you never had a hard enough push to soar into the right direction? Has your environment been a hindrance to you becoming the best that you can be? With all, some, or even isolated negative experiences, even getting a little motivated can be a mental and motivational challenge.

Will you allow your plans to fall by the wayside because it would be too difficult at this point to get back on the right track, with so many strikes against you? It's a dilemma to be sure, but not one that you cannot overcome. Can you put faith in yourself and the things that you want to accomplish?

If the answer to this question is "yes," then start today to set your mind on your short- and long-term goals. Write them down on paper so that they will be a visual reminder to you every day. Find a mentor who you know and trust. That person will be supportive of you and your goals. Your mentor cannot be a friend you hang out with. Why? Because he or she may also be standing at the same crossroads of life that you are at right now, dealing with similar unfavorable predicaments, and will not be able to help form a plan of action for you. Their desire to keep you as a friend, and their lack of life experience, will not make them very good advisors for the weighty choices that you must make. The decisions that you need to make now have to do with getting the education or work skills that you need and to get to a different and better place in life.

If regular school is out of the question, why not consider an alternate route to school by first getting your GED? Many of the community colleges and learning centers in your area will have classes in which you can enroll. There, you will get back into the habit of studying, taking and passing exams, and having the feeling of accomplishment. This will give you more confidence in yourself. You will also meet associates who are goal-oriented and making new starts in life as well. They will give you the motivation to stick to the plans that you have made. Unlike your former classmates, who attended school because it was a requirement, these associates of various ages and genders have made the choice to return to a specific program of instruction. You will find a different atmosphere here. The surroundings will be much more conducive to effective learning.

Getting your GED will also not take very long, so deciding your next step should already be in the planning stage. Will you continue on to a two- or four-year college, or will you apply yourself to learning a skill in a trade school that will afford you profitable employment? If your choice is trade school, just think—in a few months you can be doing what you dreamed of years ago and more.

Once you are employed, you will need to keep updated on the advances that take place in your field. This means that in the future you may need to take more classes. You want to make sure that you remain in the job pool and continue to be employable.

Will you be faced with discouragement? You bet you will! You might wonder why you decided to challenge yourself to such a degree. Doubting yourself sometime is to be expected. But giving up should not be in your thoughts. Talk to your mentor. Remember, that person has an interest in your success. Tell him about your self-doubt. He will give you a boost of confidence and put you back where you need to be.

Here is a good example of how a mentor can help you:

If you were driving alone down the street and your car suddenly stopped, you would get out and try to steer and push the car at the same time to move it out of the way of traffic. You might shout out for help. Or someone seeing your dilemma from the sidewalk might volunteer to assist you. That person might suggest that you get back into the driver's seat and take over the steering, while they do the pushing. The two of you working together could now get the car to a safe place. This illustrates what takes place when you are stuck in the rut of doubt and fear, and are in great need of a push to get you started again.

Sometime you will need to ask for help. Other times your chosen mentor may perceive from afar that you need a gentle push. Get back into the driver's seat and accept the help that is given. In no time at all you will be back on your way to fulfilling all of your plans. Sometimes, even the most optimistic person can feel unsure.

After getting back on the right path, how can you help others to get to where you are?

Like a swimmer who is trying to get to safety, along with other swimmers who have not yet mastered the skill, you may not be able to reach out too early in your transformation to help others to get to a safe place. But, by keeping their eyes fixed on you and your arrival to safety, they can imitate the way you maneuvered to make it to the shore. Once you are on the shore, you must make sure that your feet are firmly anchored so as not to lose your footing by throwing out a rope to others too soon. Someone whose grasp is very strong could cause you to lose your balance, and you may then be pulled back into what you are trying to avoid.

Peer pressure is very strong among young people. The desire to be different from others is not what teenagers set out to do. Conforming, or doing everything possible to fit in, is their main interest. So be aware of this pitfall to your goals. The adjustments that you are making may seem premature.

Take into account your neighborhood and how it may be different from others. Then you will understand why you must make a decision now. The incentive to attend a college or even to work on a regular job may not be the topic of conversation of most of the people you talk to on a regular basis.

Doing and planning illegal activities may be the norm for most in your surroundings. Your aim to make it outside of your circumstances will possibly go against the grain of non-planners and poor thinkers alike. But keep reminding yourself that you are on your way to becoming a real man, a man who has planned and directed his life in a new direction, a man who can pull his pants up with pride knowing that he has worked hard at what he has accomplished, and has earned the respect that accompanies his efforts.

In later years, your complaint will not be "my back-ground was not conducive to me getting ahead" or "I did not achieve because my grandparents were slaves" or "I denied the job because I am a minority, or because I am African-American or Latino." With so many opportunities available now, excuses like those will not carry very much weight in the future. So plan well and know that good planning and hard work will keep you in pace with others who are making giant strides.

Name five things you will achieve through your education (i.e., good job, raised self-esteem, feeling of accomplishment, etc.)

_____

_____

_____

_____

_____

_____

_____

_____

_____

_____

_____

_____

_____

_____

_____

_____

_____

_____

_____

_____

_____

_____

_____

CHAPTER 5

Family

No matter what you've done for yourself or for humanity, if you can't look back on having given love and attention to your own family, what have you really accomplished? —Lee Iacocca

WHAT IS A FAMILY, and why is it one of the best groups to be a part of? Our home and family is the place and people that we go to when we need to escape and get relief from the outside world. Our families can help us to make sense of what would otherwise be chaos. It is the soft place to fall when everything around you seems too difficult. A loving family will wrap their arms around you and give you the assurance that everything will be fine, even in situations that seem so entangled that solving them seems impossible. "We are in this together and whatever is needed, we are here for you." This is the kind of family unit that everyone wants to be a part of. Families are made up of a variety of groupings.

Your family may fall into one of several groups. Maybe your family is a traditional family made up of a father, mother, and siblings. Your home make-up might be a single parent family, where one parent will have the sole responsibility of running your household. A blended situation is what you might call your family because a grandmother, grandfather, aunt, uncle, cousin, or other non-relative may live under your roof and call your family theirs. No matter who the people are who are living with you, there will be just as many personalities and possibly as many problems as there are people that you must learn to deal with. This is not necessarily bad because family interactions and relationships give you early lessons on how to get along with others that you will meet and associate with later on in life.

Regardless of the way families are grouped, they will not be perfect. There will always be problems to work out and conflicts to resolve. If you have a loving household, cherish it and do not take it for granted.

Your family may be plagued by members who abuse alcohol or other substances. There may be members who are not strangers to crime and are constantly in and out of trouble. You may have older brothers, sisters, or others who make living in the home a challenge because they are not thoughtful and considerate of others who live there as well. There may be one who would rather be a lazy than a worker. Some may not respect the privacy or belongings of others. There may be others who get a kick out of verbal or physical fighting. Learning to deal with these situations may be easier said than done. In fact, it can be so hard that you may think that you would rather spend your time away from your home and family, or thoughts that are even more drastic may have crossed your mind. You may have thought at times, "I will just leave the family altogether." But think: Would leaving the home at this age create more problems than it would solve? There are important questions you should consider before that extreme step, such as "Where will I find work?" "Do I have the skills to get a good a job that will take care of all of my physical needs, such as food, shelter and clothing?" "Who would hire someone my age?" "Will renting an apartment be a problem for a young person my age?" "Do I know someone who has left home and is doing well on their own?" "If I am fortunate enough to get an apartment and a job, what will happen if I lose my job and cannot pay the rent?" "What kind of changes would sickness bring?" "How will I continue my education?"

Answering these questions will give you some insight as to what it means to be on your own. Of course, there might be a situation where it may be necessary for you to leave the family home to live with a relative. Remember, you are still a part of another family and the same rules apply for making the household one of peace and harmony wherever you live. Cooperation or non-cooperation in areas where you and others co-exist can determine how your household will run. When you see or visit the homes of friends where there is a great deal of harmony, you can be assured that this is a family that has learned the key to working together for the benefit of all involved. If you do not live in peaceful surroundings, you may wish that you belonged to that loving family who has it all worked out. You may envy the relation-ships that exist among family members in other house-holds because it is lacking in your own. What you may not know is that even seemingly perfect families have problems, too; they have just found a better way to work through the difficult issues. Therefore, they are not to be envied, but their system of problem-solving is one to learn from and to imitate.

The structure of your family may very well be set for now and may be impossible to change. However, it can be improved upon if each family member—or even if just some of them—are helpful and supportive, with eve-ryone having the desire to see a happier household take shape.

You should not feel responsible for each person's ac-tion in the family. But you can work hard on yourself to be as cooperative as possible with your parents and oth-ers, so as not to be the cause of any discord. If you have younger siblings or household members, they are watch-ing you. They are like little sponges, soaking up every-thing that they see and hear around them. How you work together within the family unit will greatly influ-ence them, either in a positive or negative way.

The more the family members cooperate with each other, the happier the family will be as a whole. Even the young will benefit and thrive in this type of atmosphere. Like you, they will be learning practical skills that they can use now and later in life.

Let's look at some of the interactions that you may have in the family that can either help or hinder family unity. Are you a helper in your home or do you sit back and enjoy the fruits of the labor of others? Do you volunteer to help with chores if you are not being paid to do so? Do you have hobbies or other interests that come before helping out in the home and doing your share in making the home run smoothly? Are you constantly asking for things that are not affordable and could possibly put a strain on the family budget? Do you compare another family's financial status with that of your family? Do you try to make your parents feel guilty about not giving you things?

Putting a guilt trip on parents because they are not able to afford certain things for you is neither fair nor loving. Should not thankfulness be a consideration? Parents do so many things for their children without asking for anything in return. What they need and should get from you is cooperation, respect, obedience, and love. You can do this without any cost or much effort.

This information will be priceless when it comes to forming your new family, that happy family that you know can be watched and copied. You can also take note and carry the good things from your present family into the new family that you will someday form. All of the negative things that you disliked, you can eliminate (i.e., screaming, physical/mental abuse and drug/alcohol use). Stressing family values, honesty, and commitment is what you will teach your children, because that is what you have practiced.

On the other hand, because of the hurt that it may have caused to your family and others in the neighborhood, you may determine that abusing alcohol or the use and sale of illegal substances will not be tolerated in your neighborhood or in your home.

You may decide that all of your future offspring will reside in the home that you head, and will not be spread out among many homes and many women. You may also decide that none of your children will have to depend others for financial support. You may choose to instill the value of family, honest work, and accomplishment. What a wonderful family to be a part of and what an outstanding man you will have become!

What do you want for yourself and your family?

_____

_____

_____

_____

_____

_____

_____

Bernice Harris

What steps do *you* need to take to acquire it?

_____

_____

_____

_____

_____

_____

_____

_____

CHAPTER 6

Friends

The only way to have a friend, is to be one. —*Ralph Waldo Emerson*

DURING YOUR LIFETIME, you will meet many acquaintances. A few of these will go on to become your good friends. The kind of friendship you enjoy with your good friends will be different. With some, you will just enjoy hanging around with them, and sometimes doing things together. With others, you will enjoy a closer relationship; you will share many feelings of both joy and disappointment. You will share many intimate details about yourself that you do not share with anyone else. Your good friend, on the other hand, will trust you with their most guarded secrets.

Some friendships that are made during your early years will be discontinued because of misunderstandings, moving to a different location, growth in a different direction, or a variety of other reasons. Some friendships will survive into adulthood and become stronger as the years go by.

In the process of making friends, your parents will probably have a say about the friends that you are making. If they feel that a friend you are spending a great deal of time with is not a good person for you to be around, they will voice that. They may even explain to you certain traits that they see in your friend that would put your good qualities at risk. Keep your ears and mind open to your parents' concerns about the friends that you are selecting. They have good insight into the people, personalities, and things that could be harmful to you.

On the other hand, you may choose a friend that your parents are very fond of. Your friend could become like another family member, well respected and loved. You would also have the same kind of acceptance into your friend's family. What will you look for in a friend? Will you look for someone exactly like yourself or will you recognize that even though you have many things in common with that person, each of you are different and one of a kind, and there are things that you will have different views on?

Is that what you want your friend to understand about you, too? Maybe you have not yet made a good friend because you are shy and not very good at starting a conversation. Or you may be very good at speaking with others, but have not found another person to be friends with who is compatible in age or interest. You should not settle for hanging out with just anyone, for the sake of being around another person, just because you do not want to spend time alone. If the person or persons who you are spending time with have questionable conduct, alone time can be good for doing a self-search, really getting to know yourself. When a friend does come along, you will know much more about yourself and can bring more to a friendship.

With the new change in your life, the friends that you now have may choose not to have you as a friend anymore when you inform them that you will be going on a different course. Either they will join you in becoming a better, more productive person or they will not want to spend much time with you at all.

Spending time with a person who wants to re-direct his life will give them a different view of you, which it should. Their thinking could be that you will not be a fun person to be around any longer and they may decide to stay away from you altogether. Instead of having fun with you, they may make fun of you. That is okay.

That will free you without too much conflict to move on in another direction. Even if you have to wait for that best friend to come along, it will be well worth waiting for.

Remember that special friend when they do come into your life, they will be open to listening to your problems, sharing your happiness, and just being there for you.

You will be the same kind of comfort and pleasurable person for them. Will you have to spend long days, weeks, months, or years looking for that special friend? No! One day it will just happen, and you will have that friend. You will try to think back to how the friendship really got started. It may even bring a chuckle at the ease that the friendship was formed and continued. You will not have to ask that special person to be your friend. The friendship will come and flourish through a few or several interactions.

Make sure that your friend is positive and encouraging and has the same desire to do well in life. You will now have a friend's shoulder to lean on, but this should not be at the expense of pushing your family aside because you feel that your friend understands you better. In strong homes, families love, understand, and support members of the household. Each one understands that friends do not replace family.

You will know the friend is positive and encouraging if a situation like this arises:

You are having difficulty in algebra, or are concerned about some other test coming up that you are convinced you cannot pass. A good friend will either help you to study for the exam or encourage you to study hard and not to give up.

A friend who does not have your best interests may confirm your doubts, and even encourage you to skip class and hang out at the mall or some other fun place. A continued relationship with a person like that will eventually change the good habits you have formed.

Not everything that comes out of your friend's mouth may be positive, but if you are hearing more negative words than positive ones, BEWARE!

Who are your closest friends and acquaintances? Share
what you like about them.

_____

_____

_____

_____

_____

_____

_____

What do *you* think makes a good friend?

_____

_____

_____

_____

_____

_____

_____

CHAPTER 7

The Neighborhood

Be not afraid of growing slowly, be afraid of standing still. —*Chinese Proverb*

Drugs, gangs, crime, nightly gunfire, drive-by shootings, young lives snuffed out, abandoned buildings, littered streets, multiple families under one roof, poor schools, lack of interest in education, young unwed mothers, absent fathers, needy children, inadequate health care, joblessness, homelessness, hopelessness...and the list goes on.

Some or all of these things may be what you encounter each day as you go about daily life in your neighborhood. Growing up in an area with so many minuses and so few pluses can be tough. It can be hard to safely walk around and carry out the things that you need or want to do.

Walking to school or through the park, enjoying the beauty of nature, can pose a risk to your safety. Riding a bus to take in an evening movie or sitting on your front steps with friends or even relaxing by the window with a good book can put you in danger of being harmed by gunfire.

You may recall incidents where small children lost their lives in drive-by shootings because they wanted to do something as simple as going outside to play. The child happened to be in the wrong place at the wrong time. Living in an area like this calls for good survival skills, the kind of survival skills that have been compared to being in combat or living in a jungle with dangerous predators, where caution has to be taken at all times. It is necessary to learn protective measures if you want to stay neutral and safe in an area where pressure is put on young men to join or participate in activities of which you may need to stay clear.

None of this is said to frighten you or to turn you into a hermit who never ventures outside of the home to enjoy life and friends. Instead, it is a precaution to be careful with whom and how you move and associate within your neighborhood.

You should not want to hang out with the known troublemakers in your neighborhood. Even if you do not do the things that these individuals are involved in, you could be harmed by associating with persons whose conduct and activities are questionable. This precaution is necessary if you want to make it into adulthood with all of your plans intact.

You may have spent some time outside of your neighborhood. You have no doubt noticed that neighborhoods can differ according to the people who live there. Some neighborhoods are pleasant to live in, without many noticeable problems, and serious crimes are infrequent. Residents are free to move around and do things with much more freedom than if they lived in a high-crime area.

Maybe you have the desire to live in a better, safer neighborhood, one with more freedom and fewer restrictions.

Your thoughts might center on the day that you will acquire a good-paying job and can move the family into a beautiful neighborhood and a nice comfortable home that everyone will love and enjoy. That goal certainly is possible, if you are willing to work hard and if you are a good, careful life planner with your focus kept on your goals.

In many ways, your neighborhood is like your family. You spend large amounts of time there. You probably are acquainted with a number of people who reside there as well. You know the good and bad sides of your neighbors. It is also likely the place where most of your friends live, go to school, and hang out. Regardless of where you may go on a daily basis, eventually you will make your way back home to the neighborhood. Many of the people in your neighborhood are completely satisfied living there, regardless of the existing conditions. They may not have the motivation to move on or to do anything better with their lives. Perhaps they have not been shown a better way. Maybe they have been shown a different way, but the old way is easier and takes much less effort. A number of young people in your neighborhood may be far-sighted enough to see that there are possibilities beyond their present situation. These individuals will choose another direction to a new and more constructive life through school, job training, and work. Other young men, in their desire to acquire a huge amount of money very fast, may want to make a leap into sports or some segment of the entertainment world, not realizing that few people, even with great talents, make it into the big time. They want the stylish clothes and the lifestyle of the rich and famous NOW!

These luxurious things are desirable. However, few make good, solid realistic plans to acquire them through honest work or other legal means. If the big money does not come quickly enough, a shortcut to the fast big money is sometimes taken. Getting into unlawful activities, such as selling drugs and dealing in stolen or illegal merchandise, could possibly be the preferred way to get the "better things in life." These methods of getting money will surely bring on more problems than they solve.

How many people do you know who have made the decision to take up life as a lawbreaker and then go on to fame and fortune? Do you know anyone from your neighborhood who has spent time in the city jail or has been sent away to prison and then has come back to do great things? It is indeed possible to come to one's senses at any point in life, and change into a better, more productive person. This is possible for you and everyone you know.

Consider Judge Greg Mathis who presides over a weekly television courtroom. He very openly admits that a portion of his early life was not good. However, he made the decision to change. His change was extraordinary. With a new outlook, he went back to school, finished law school, passed the bar, and became a judge. Today he inspires millions to lead a more useful life and to live up to their full potential. Now, instead of standing before a judge, he is the judge!

You may think of one or two exceptions in your neighborhood that started on a very reckless road and did a complete turn-around, too. Some of these young men may have spent as much time on the inside of prison walls as on the outside, and the desire to do a change for the better has not been a passing thought. Doing good things for their family has lost its importance. Instead of making an easier, happier life for the family, the family probably has been plunged into deeper poverty by paying to get the lawbreaker out of trouble.

As you observe your neighborhood, you will come to realize that you are not the neighborhood and the neighborhood is not you. You are a resident in your neighborhood and you can do things differently than the people who live there. Your life does not have to be molded by the patterns that others have shaped, especially if the pattern is not a positive one.

You are young and capable! You have the ability to draw up your own constructive life plans and to see them through to completion. The most poverty-stricken neighborhood can produce dreamers that can see beyond their present condition and make a difference in their life and the lives of others as well.

Begin today to think as an individual. Let your good thoughts move you forward, and not backwards to a place that is comfortable, familiar, and easy. You will never make it to your destination by going backwards or staying in the same place. You must make forward movement toward your goal even if the movement is slow in the beginning.

Think outside of where you are today. If your new way of thinking is not popular, and if you are not getting the support or the go-ahead from others to go down a path that is different, unknown, or untraveled by many of your neighborhood peers, then are you willing to try it on your own?

To get others to join you on your journey to change may be similar to the children's story of The Little Red Hen. Do you remember the story? There is a moral to this story, see if you can find it.

The Little Red Hen, while scratching for seed, found a grain of wheat that could benefit all of her friends: the duck, the dog, and the cat. The only thing that she needed was a little help from them, from planting the grain of wheat and cutting the wheat when it was ready for harvesting, to threshing and taking it to the mill to be ground into flour and baked into bread for all of them to eat. These were very easy tasks if everyone had cooperated and had the same goals in mind: to eventually sit down and enjoy a fine meal. However, none of the barnyard friends had the foresight to see further than the small task that they were asked to do.

But when the Little Red Hen went to each of her friends—the Duck, the Dog, and the Cat—to ask which of them could help get the wheat ready for eating, each answered "not I." "Then I will do it myself," she would reply. And she did! Finally, the day came when the wheat was made into flour, and the flour was made into delicious bread.

"Who will help me eat the bread?" asked the Little Red Hen. "I will," said the Dog, "I will," said the Cat, and "I will," said the Duck. "No, no," said the Little Red Hen, "I will eat it all by myself," and she did.

Did you get the moral of the story? Did it encourage you to do what you need to do whether others in your neighborhood see how some actions today could benefit them in the future? Can you imitate the Little Red Hen by going ahead and working to realize your goals?

On your destination to attain your goals, you do not want to overlook a part of life that is very necessary for success and happiness—the spiritual aspect to life. It is as important, if not more important, than the physical and emotional parts of you. It is not searched for and found, but without it, whatever accomplishment you may attain in life will be fulfilling. There will always be an empty spot that begs to be filled. The spiritual part of a person is lacking when you see people with all of the job success and money, and they are still unhappy and unfulfilled. When you learn the real way to success, you can be the motivator to those who are hesitant to take that first step into the future. They have seen the possibilities through you. They, too, can tread out into the darkness of the unknown, and into the brightness of a new day filled with new experiences and successes.

What goes on in your neighborhood?

_____

_____

_____

_____

_____

_____

_____

What changes would you like to see made?

_____

_____

_____

_____

_____

_____

_____

How can you contribute to those changes?

_____

_____

_____

_____

_____

_____

_____

_____

CHAPTER 8

Honor and Respect

Respect for ourselves guides our morals; respect for others guides our manners. —Laurence Sterne

RESPECT AND HONOR are two words that have almost disappeared from the habits and lives of many young people today. Respect and honor have been replaced by rudeness, bad manners, vulgar and offensive speech, and just plain impoliteness. The older generation must take some of the blame for the loss of good manners in today's youth. Adults have not always remembered what they were taught about respect and honor. Therefore, there has been a gap in the teaching and modeling of these valuable traditions. A failure to teach and to show by doing has left a serious break in the much-needed human-to-human interaction today. Teachings on how to treat, respect, and even to honor a person is in the distant past.

Your wish to become a different person must include a return to those old values. Regardless of what you do with your life, a coarse and impolite person is never taken to very well. Even if you put on the best clothes and have the greatest talents, you will possibly be remembered more for how you come off to people than how you dress or for your abilities and talents.

You may have heard people discussing their bosses. If the boss is a person who does not show respect to the employees and if he is rude and inconsiderate, that is what you will hear talked about, both inside and outside of the office. The boss may be a graduate of Yale or Harvard and have the potential for great leadership, but if these abilities are not mixed with respect, there will be an unpleasant climate in the workplace. The boss will not be happy because he gets little respect, the employees will not be happy because they are not respected, and so goes the peace of the office. The same conditions can exist in a home where respect is not given or received.

If you are not sure how to earn respect for yourself or how to show it to others, the following can be helpful.

Self-Respect

In this context, we will define self-respect as boundaries that you set for yourself on values that you hold dear, and boundaries that will not be lowered on a whim by you or others. After you have set these definite standards, you will not let another person's view of you affect those standards just to keep a friendship, or not to stand out as being different.

Are you frequently tempted to do things that will have an effect on how you will later feel about yourself or how you will be viewed by others? Are you getting the respect that you want from people of all ages? Does your dress and manners give evidence to everyone that you respect yourself and them as well? Do you get more gentle smiles or do you get more stares that says "in your presence I had better watch out because you might cause me harm?"

What about your abilities? Maybe you are very good at doing certain things, but you undervalue your skills. Or you may not do some things well and you may boast that you can do them. Neither of these are good. Try to find an unassuming attitude that is not too much of either over or under-evaluating yourself. Over-evaluating yourself puts you in the position of being a show-off or an attention getter. You may get attention, but it will not be the kind you are seeking. Under achieving is not good because that can prevent you from reaching your full potential. You may always be in doubt about your ability to do things that you are fully capable of doing. Your accomplishments and abilities should never be flaunted by you. Praise that is given to you should not be from your mouth, but the mouths of others. Over-appraising yourself could cause you to get more disrespect than respect. All of the changes that you are making are for you, but they will also affect your relationship with others. You would not necessarily go out of your way to make enemies by being unpleasant. You should not be so eager to make friends that you occasionally sit on the fence, or cross over it, after you have determined that your life is to be one of good morals, honesty, truthfulness, and other good qualities. If you do not feel that standing on a street corner with teens whose conversation and actions drifts toward things that you have told yourself that you will never do, then self-respect should move you to distance yourself from that group. Self-respect compromised in any way can lead to feelings of guilt. As a teen that is constantly in the company of peers, you will be faced with situations that will test your resolve. Stay true to yourself and to your values. If that makes you proud today, in the future your happiness will be multiplied many times when you look back over your life and see that good resolves which are followed bring wonderful results!

Respect for Parents

It should be a natural thing for a teen to respect the wisdom of his or her parents. This should be easy if the child recognizes the amount of knowledge the parents have gained in years of living and observing life. They embarked into parenthood with a lack of experience in child rearing. As you grew up, in small stages and through trial and error, they figured out an awesome project. If your parents read parenting books about child rearing, at some point the books had to be laid aside and they had to deal with any real, one-of-a-kind problems that involved you. Because everyone is so different, your brothers and sisters may have had their own problems. Therefore, dealing with and solving a variety of problems provides experience that is not easily forgotten. It would be impossible to go through years of child rearing without gaining a great measure of knowledge. If you have learned to have appreciation for the role, concerns, and the wisdom of your parents, you are far ahead of some of your peers.

Many young men today may feel that their parents or caregivers should not be respected because they do not give respect. Others may reason that no respect is due because too much is known about their parents' lives. The parent may use foul language. His or her behavior may not be what you would desire in a parent. They may abuse alcohol or drugs, or may even be serving time in prison. In many other ways they may not have been very good in their role of modeling and giving love and good parenting to their children.

The children may have suffered from neglect and their care may have been delegated to someone else. Other relatives and even foster parents may have stepped up to give you the parenting that you needed. Do you show the proper respect for those fill-in parents? The actions of a parent with problems may hide a story that is mingled with emotional hurt and disappointments. Trying to conceal such unhappy experiences can show up in vices such as drugs and alcohol, to which a parent may have become enslaved. A child would certainly not be in a position to make changes in an individual, and should not feel guilty because of the inability to cure adult dilemmas.

Some problems are deep-seated and much too complicated for children to know what to do. Much professional help may be needed before a person can function normally. If any of this applies to you, what can you do?

Respectfully talk to that parent about the concerns that you have. Even in showing them that you are trying to understand will relieve some of the hard feelings that you have bottled up inside. It would not be easy to have compassion for a person and at the same time be disrespectful toward them.

Work at this a little at a time, and with maturity and time, your resentment should slowly melt away. Understanding the plight that you and your parents are in can be like a soothing cream on a sore spot. It may not instantly cure the spot, but it can make it feel better until it is completely healed.

If you have parents that have always been there for you, and you have not suffered as a result of neglect or other reason, then you should give them even more honor and respect. You do not want to be a know-it-all when you interact with your parents on important issues, but you should listen and apply the tidbits about life that are being passed onto you.

Do not push for too much freedom now. More freedom will come with time. If you push for too much freedom and misuse it, it can put you in a situation where you could lose it in the future.

On occasion, your parents' response to something that you may feel strongly about may be "no." That does not mean that they want to make you feel miserable and deprive you of a good time. What it does mean is that they want you to be around to enjoy many good times in the future. So do not confuse withholding certain things from you—or maybe not permitting you to do them at all—as hate.

Hate would be just the opposite of what they are trying to do to protect you. If they hated you, they would tolerate and encourage all kinds of unacceptable behavior, knowing that life would turn out badly for you. They would be happy to know that your life would be a disaster. What happens in the next decades of your life would be of little interest to them.

Would you respect a parent who you later found out held back helpful information from you that would have led you to have a better life, even though you resisted it and did not understand the reasoning behind it at the time? Hands-off parenting may seem to be the best way to go now.

However, ten years from now, when you have grown up and may be a parent yourself, you will see the wisdom in all of it. You will understand that life is so complicated, that trial and error is not the best way to learn or to gain experience.

Bear in mind that there are boundaries and laws that all of us must respect. No one is exempt from answering to someone, not even your parents! Look at the prison population, with numerous young men behind bars.

They did not like boundaries and did not like answering to anyone. They pushed the limits and ended up with all kinds of restrictions and boundaries, and in many cases, for life.

Wouldn't you rather have limits set by someone who has shown you that they love and care for you, and have done a super job so far in steering you down the right path? Will you now show respect for them and allow them to help you over the next few years of your life to become a real man? Can you respect and honor them?

Respect for Women

Mothers, grandmothers, sisters, aunts, female friends, and women in general should be respected. Restoring respect in your everyday association with women actually comes down to just being thoughtful. Respect for women and others at one time was called "being courteous." Being courteous should not be out of style, but should be what a young man wants to show when dealing with the opposite sex.

This would include those simple everyday contacts like opening doors and allowing a female companion, or any other woman who is entering a door at the same time as you, to enter into the room in front of you while you are holding the door for them to enter. Respect and honor would mean that a young man would make sure that his female companion is sitting before he takes a seat, even pulling the chair out for her. If it becomes necessary for you to leave a table while dining, an "excuse me" before leaving is proper.

If you are in a crowded room or on public transportation, you should give up your seat for a standing woman, regardless of her age. Have you noticed some young men diving for the first vacant seat without giving consideration to a standing woman, even an elderly one? In the past, men would respect women by avoiding profanity in their presence. It was a no-no to speak foul language in the earshot of a woman. If that kind of speech slipped out accidentally while in a woman's presence, many apologies would be forthcoming. Do you hear apologies coming from your peers or other males when they accidentally use inappropriate speech in the presence of women? Or is it more common to hear shocking speech used to seem more hip and important to women?

Do you disrespect women by improper touching? A woman's body belongs to her and should not be an object of uninvited contact. The excuse that "the way she is dressed invites certain attention" is not good reasoning. Her poor judgment in dress could be looked at in the same way as your wearing of the sagging pants and hoodies. The clothes may be speaking a falsehood about the wearer. Has the demeaning of women in hip-hop songs caused you to show less and less respect for women? Has the four- and five-letter words used for females become a part of your vocabulary too? Never feel that you can listen to those negative implants without some of them taking up residency in your head and becoming a part of your vocabulary, whether you intend to be influenced or not.

In coming years, you will probably marry and have a family. You will not think of your beautiful caring wife, the mother of your children, as one of those shocking substitute words for a woman. You would surely be enraged if a young man referred to her or your innocent daughter in that way. It would not be appropriate, then, for you to call someone else such names, or listen to them used, even in the context of a song. Keep in mind that *all* women are a part of someone's family and should be respected.

Even the gentlest man will challenge anyone to a fight who spoke in a disrespectful way about his mother. Talking rudely about someone's mother is not another way to have fun and to make jokes (playing the dozens.) This kind of entertainment is not good for a young man who is making positive changes in his life. So if you do not speak of women in those shameful ways when you have conversations with your friends, do not allow a singer to change your moral values through the lyrics of a song.

Do not be willing to pay out dollars for someone to negatively brainwash you, while at the same time changing your new value system. Your goal is to have more respect for women, not less.

Respect for Everyone

It would be very difficult to think of someone who should not be respected. Teachers, police officers, older people, employers, and others in authority are due respect. Do you have offensive names for the police? Is the name that you call him when you are talking with your friends the same name that you would call him if you were speaking to him directly? When dealing with older people, do you speak with them in the same way that you speak to your friends, in street jargon that would be hard for them to understand? How often are you using words like "please," "thank you," or "excuse me?"

Are you making others a captive audience when it comes to the type and the volume of the music that you listen to? Do you realize that people have different tastes in music? When you are in public places, you meet a variety of music lovers. It shows disrespect for others to force them to become a captive audience to your taste in music, at a volume that they probably do not appreciate. Can you play and enjoy your music inside of your home or some other place that will not disturb others? Even music played inside of the home should show respect for other family members and your neighbors.

Young children are people, too, and they should also be respected. You might recall someone older than you who took time with you when you were very young. He or she showed respect for your young thoughts and feelings, and did not push you away when you had questions that needed answers. Small children have feelings that they are unable to express due to limited life experience. Their vocabulary is also limited. In time, their vocabulary, along with an increased understanding, will surface. Then they will be able to express themselves just like you.

So, if you become irritated with them, you do not want to push them or give them a whack on the side of the head. Even if you were not treated with respect by others when you were younger, you have all the more reason to respect someone else who is young, because you are aware of what it feels like when you are small and not respected.

Respect is also due to the students at your school and people you might meet in other places who have handicaps or some other disorder that makes them different from most of the population. These people would welcome a "hello" or a warm smile, rather than a stare and a "hey man, what happened to you?" Is that not the way you would want to be treated if you were in their situation?

If you live in a city, you may encounter homeless people on the street. In some places, teens have made it commonplace to beat up these citizens who do not have a traditional place to live, a permanent home. They might feel that they are less of a person than other people because of their condition. Even homeless people should not have their dignity taken away by cruel words and actions.

Many of the homeless are not suffering by choice, but by some unfortunate circumstance that came into their life that did not have a quick solution. Underneath the layers of dirty clothing and dirty bodies, a real, feeling individual exists. There is a real heart inside of them that loves, hurts, and is saddened by hurtful remarks and heartless actions that further add to their misery.

Respect for Property

Whether you live in the best neighborhood or the worst neighborhood, where you live is someone's property. The property may belong to your family or someone else may own it. The place where you reside must be respected. Property is respected by taking care of it and by not adopting the "I don't care" attitude about its condition because it does not belong to you.

"I didn't spend money on where I live, so I will not take an interest in it" and "I am waiting until I am an adult and I will buy that big beautiful house with everything in place" may be the thinking of some. The opposite view should be "I will learn how to care for and respect where I live now, and when I get into another surrounding, I will really know how to take care of it."

The latter kind of thinking will make you mindful of not only keeping the inside of your home in good shape, but to also make sure that you are not deliberately ruining the outside, whether it belongs to someone else or to your family.

In many neighborhoods you will see graffiti on the sides of apartment buildings and garages, broken-down porch rails, and broken windows destroyed by carelessness. You will also see broken bottles and litter of all kinds in the street. If everyone walked the few steps to the garbage can to discard their potato chip bags, candy wrappers, and pop bottles, think of the change that it could bring to a neighborhood! When you show respect in all of these areas, you will have reached a milestone in your development. You are now very close to becoming the person that you could not ever have dreamed of.

Who do you have a great deal of respect for and why?

_____

_____

_____

_____

_____

_____

_____

How can you apply some of their good qualities into your own life?

_____

_____

_____

_____

_____

_____

_____

_____

CHAPTER 9

Money

A penny saved is a penny earned. —*Benjamin Franklin*

WE GET OUR FIRST PERCEPTION of money from an early age. As a small boy, you may remember being given money. Maybe the money was a paper dollar or small coins that jingled in your pocket. Whatever the denomination of the money, it boosted your self-importance. You knew that the money could be exchanged for things. You could buy an ice cream cone, a candy bar, or your favorite magazine. You also had another option. You could put it away in your piggy bank, add to it, and allow it to multiply. You would then be able to either buy a larger treat for yourself, or you could leave the money there and watch it grow.

With age, your understanding of how money works in the real world grew through other experiences. Perhaps you played the game of Monopoly or some other game where a player loses money, springs back, and eventually makes enough money to win over the opponents. In real life, the opponent is YOU. How you handle your finances will determine whether you handle this portion of your life as well as you are learning to master the other parts of your life.

Although money is necessary for survival, it does not hold the key to happiness. Money does not define the inner character or your worth. Whether you have a lot of it or a little, it does not speak of your morals, principles, or integrity. You are the same person inside regardless of how much money you have. To become a different person, you must work on that apart from what you acquire or do not acquire financially.

In this chapter, we will discuss how you can make a conscious decision to save a portion of the money that you acquire through an allowance or work and how to handle credit in a responsible way. Acquiring money through an allowance, work, or through saving is the very best way to acquire money. However, some young people find this way too slow, so they will risk their life, a police record, and their freedom to get the big, fast money.

This is an unsatisfactory way for acquiring money. If a stint in prison or a police record is made as a result of illegal activities in your youth, this record will follow you into adulthood. It will not matter that you are now older and know a much better way of handling your life. The bad record that you made when you were young will not go away. It will follow you and will affect your life when it comes to getting a job, and could even get in the way of you easily obtaining credit to buy that new home and car, even if you made changes in your life a long time ago.

We live in a very materialistic, money-driven society. More than ever, you and your peers are being bombarded with advertising that promotes everything from what you should be driving, listening to, wearing, drinking, and eating to what you should be buying in general.

Your favorite entertainer may even promote some of these items. Do you make the decision to purchase items because they look really cool in a commercial, or because someone in the entertainment world is wearing it or is a spokesperson for the item, without giving thought to whether you or your parents can afford it? What you may not know is that a common practice in the entertainment world is for designers to loan items of clothing and jewelry to stars without cost to them when they are making public appearances at red carpet or other events.

The star looks good (for free) and the designer or company receives (free) advertising for their clothing or jewelry. Consumers like what they see and go out to buy the products that the stars are using, but they have to pay for them. Most youngsters do not have enough money to compete with what celebrities are receiving for free.

Should you have the desire for nice things? There is nothing wrong with getting nice things that you can comfortably afford. However, you want to be sure that you are not buying things just because others are wearing it, or to show that you can afford something when, in truth, neither you nor your parents can afford many of the things you want.

It is not necessary to spend every dime that comes into your possession. You must also put some money away for things that you will need in the future. Have you had the experience where you had a considerable amount of money and spent it on one item that quickly lost its newness and appeal? Did you later wish that you had spent less on the one item, and divided the money into purchasing several things that you could have enjoyed? Or did you wish that you had made the decision not to purchase the item at all?

Do a little calculation as to how saved money can grow. If you start to save $1 every day of the year starting on January 1, by December 31 (the year's end) you will have saved $365. You may say that $1 a day is too much, as you may not have that much to spare. Well, what about one half that amount, fifty cents? At the end of one month that has 31 days in it, you will have saved $15.50 by putting aside fifty cents every day. By the year's end, that amount will add up to $182.50 if you hid it in a sock, or put it in a bank in your home. If you deposit the money into a commercial bank in a passbook savings account, the bank will pay you a small amount of interest on each dollar that you deposit, adding even more to what you have saved.

If you are asking "how will I get the money to save if I do not get an allowance or if I do not have a job?" The answer is simple: learn how to make money with your talents. Almost everyone has a talent that, if he or she thought hard enough about it, could be used to make money. For some, it will be very easy to determine the talent, while others may struggle initially in figuring out what they can do especially well, or what skill they can acquire to make extra money. If you have decided what your talent is, you need to polish it so that you can get others to pay you for using it.

For example, if you are good at using the computer, you may decide to offer in-home classes to friends and neighbors for a fee that is reasonable and equal to your skill. What about your neighbor down the street who has a new computer that is sitting and collecting dust because he or she does not know how to use it? Are they aware of all of the functions that can be done on the computer?

For that neighbor, and others in your neighborhood who do not know how to surf the Internet or use some of the software programs like Microsoft Word or Excel, your services can change their lives. Your clients will enjoy learning new functions and skills on their computer and you will earn extra money. Both of you will benefit from your services. Make an attractive flyer from your computer, noting the services that you offer, along with the fee for service and a telephone number where you can be contacted. You are now in business! You will need to keep a good record of your clients' names, addresses, and the services you provided to them. Also, you will need to note the date and price you charged for the service. You should also purchase an inexpensive notebook to keep track of all of your business information.

In the future, you can teach a more advanced class. For this class, you will charge a little more because you will teach more advanced techniques, such as tables and formatting, and whatever other needs that you have observed, which your clients lack during your interaction with them. Most of the essential skills that you will need to operate your computer business may be learned in school. If this is the case, you will benefit from your computer class. Ask questions about the computer functions that you do not understand. If you are self-taught, continue to explore and learn new skills. It will pay off in the future.

If your client is satisfied with your class, he or she will recommend you to family, friends, and other neighbors. You can encourage your clients to recommend your service by giving them a free or discounted class for a good word. This will create even more income for you.

Do you have the equipment to make beats? There are many people seeking inexpensive beats for their lyrics. If art is more to your interest, why not hand-decorate t-shirts and/or gym shoes or other items? If you like to work outside, car washing may interest you. If you start a business washing cars, only a few old rags and a bucket will put you in business. Mowing lawns, trimming shrubbery, and caring for flowers in the summer can bring additional satisfaction to you as you watch the things that you have cared for grow.

In the fall, you can rake leaves. In the winter, you can get more work than you can possibly do shoveling snow and salting sidewalks, if you live in an area that gets large amounts of snow. A shovel is all that is needed to start your business. When offering your services to potential clients, make sure that your service is always top-notch and your prices are comparable to your experience. An adult's advice will be very helpful in setting rates for your services.

Make your services stand out. Follow through on your word. If the agreement for your services is to start at a set time, you should be there at that time or even a little before the actual start time. This shows your client that you respect their time and your agreement.

Are you stronger in a subject than some of your classmates? Why not offer to tutor them for that difficult test that is coming up? You can also tutor students in lower grades in subjects at which you excel.

Many young boys can cut hair well. Can you do that? Would a senior citizen prefer a nice hair trim in the comfort of his home rather than venturing outside and going a farther distance through traffic to get to a barbershop? Would a busy working parent prefer their child's hair to be cared for in their home rather than spend precious time, driving, sitting and waiting in a barber shop to be serviced? You could be the answer to both of their problems if you have haircutting skills.

Your schoolmates can use your haircutting service, too. If you charged three to four dollars less than their regular barber, you will make money and your friend will have extra dollars to spend on other things. You may even run specials on certain days of the week. However you decide to run your business, just stand back and watch your client list grow.

Do not forget to dress appropriately when giving services to your clients. If your skills are good but your attire doesn't match, your clothing may deny you the opportunity to make that extra money, because your clients may not trust you as much. If you are shy or just not a people person, you can become a seller on Web sites such as Amazon, eBay, or some of the other auction sites. Just remember that your buyers are not people you know, but you must deal with them in the same way that you deal with your face-to-face clients — honestly and without deception. You must not misrepresent the condition of items that you are selling. When you promise to ship items, you must keep your word. If you do business in this way, you will build up a good reputation for being a trustworthy online seller.

These are just a few ways that can bring you extra money. With a little brainstorming, you will be able to come up with other ways to make income for yourself.

Do not forget to keep a record of your Internet clients. In addition, you want to record what you sold them, when you sold it, the price of the item, the name and address of the client, and the date the item was shipped. This is similar to the records you keep for your neighbors. You want to be a very good record keeper. If your business becomes profitable, you will be required to pay income tax on the money that you have earned.

Because of the continual additions that you are making to your account, and the interest that you are earning, the money in your passbook savings account will grow as well. You may now want to put the savings into an account that will draw more interest, like a Certificate of Deposit (CD.) In time, if you have saved well, your bank may offer you a credit card. If your parents agree that you are of age and have become responsible, they may allow you to accept the credit card with some restrictions.

All of the activity that you have on your credit card will be reported to the credit bureaus. The file that they keep on your credit card activity is called a credit report. Things that will not be good on your credit report are late or missed payments. These will result in negative marks on your credit history. It is very important that you make all payments on time, five to six days before the due date. This assures that your payment will go through the mail and get posted by the date when it is due. This should not be taken lightly. The credit that you will soon be able to obtain will follow you for a long time. If your credit history is not good, it will decrease the chance of other companies offering you more credit. When you apply for more credit, the businesses that you are applying to for credit will ask the credit bureau how you have handled the credit that has been extended to you in the past.

If your credit history is bad and you do get approved for more credit, it will be at a higher rate of interest than the people who pays on time. If you do not have good credit history, think what that would mean if you were making a large purchase like a car or home? The higher interest rate would be huge. A credit card is more than plastic; it represents your money. Just because it can be pulled out and used easily, many people do not look at it as representing money that must be paid back. So, people use credit to the limit on things that they do not need, simply because the card is so convenient to use and they are not pulling cash out of their pocket. Before they know it, many people end up deep in mountains of debt they are unable to pay. Use credit and money wisely. If you start doing so in your youth, you will form good money habits that will have lifetime benefits.

What are some things that you're good or talented at?

_____

_____

_____

_____

_____

_____

_____

What are your career goals and are they related to your talents?

_____

_____

_____

_____

_____

_____

_____

_____

Will you need to attend college, a trade school, or receive a certification in order to pursue your career goal? If so, outline the steps you need to take to achieve your goal.

_____

_____

_____

_____

_____

_____

_____

Can you begin to make money now by using your talent? If so, how?

_____

_____

_____

_____

_____

_____

_____

_____

CHAPTER 10

Putting It All Together

Even if you are on the right track, you will get run over if you just sit there. —Will Rogers

Now that we have talked about and covered many topics, how will you put this new knowledge to work?

You have learned how to find the real you amidst the labels and name that you may have been given or the way that you may have felt about yourself. You have learned that you are very unique and a special individual like none other on this earth. Obtaining this understanding should help you develop your own interests and goals without the burden of trying to imitate others whose talents and goals have led them in a different direction. Did you understand that fame and money is not the basis of happiness? You've learned that having self-esteem is important, and a certain amount of education is needed to carry you where you want to go.

Did you realize the importance of the family before you took a closer look at its structure and the cooperation and love that holds it together? Did you know that your role in the family is very important and that you can add much to its happiness by listening to and cooperating with your parents and others who are older, drawing on their years of experience and knowledge? Do you remember that selecting your friends carefully is necessary because your choice could either help or get in the way of your future plans?

How much respect and honor you owe to everyone, including yourself, may have been an eye-opener because of its lack in your life. Working a nine-to-five job may have opened an option to you that you had never even considered, as a better way of making money than the shortcut to the easy life of being a lawbreaker. Did you get the message that what you wear, and how it is worn, can make a difference in how you are perceived? The wrong conclusions can be drawn about you just by what you are wearing without you or the observer speaking a word.

Are you ready to make practical applications of what you have learned overall?

Your goals, in your own words and handwriting, will make those goals your personal ambition. As you continue reading and rereading this book, your goals and application of each step will remind you of what you have set out to do. This will be a step-by-step process for making your new transformation. Just as you did not grow to your present age in a few days, you may not perfect all of your plans in a short time either. It is a work in progress! But each step that you work on and accomplish will give you the motivation to move on to the next step. If you slip back into the old you, do not think "I've failed, so I am giving up." Failure is not a part of your plan! Do what you need to do to get redirected and get back on the track that you have started. Soon you and others will see the changes that you have made. Before you know it, the man that you look at in the mirror is really you. Every inch of you has become a real man. Hats off, and pants up, you have made it!

Please answer the following questions:

(1) What did you learn from reading this book?

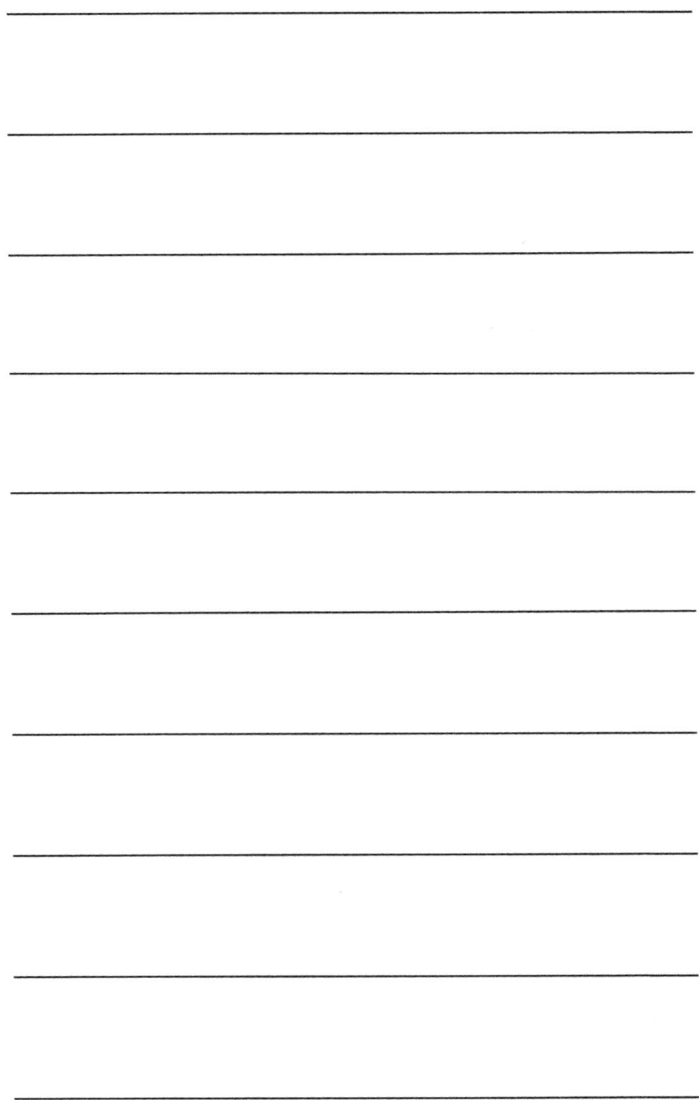

(2) How will you apply what you've learned?

_____

_____

_____

_____

_____

_____

_____

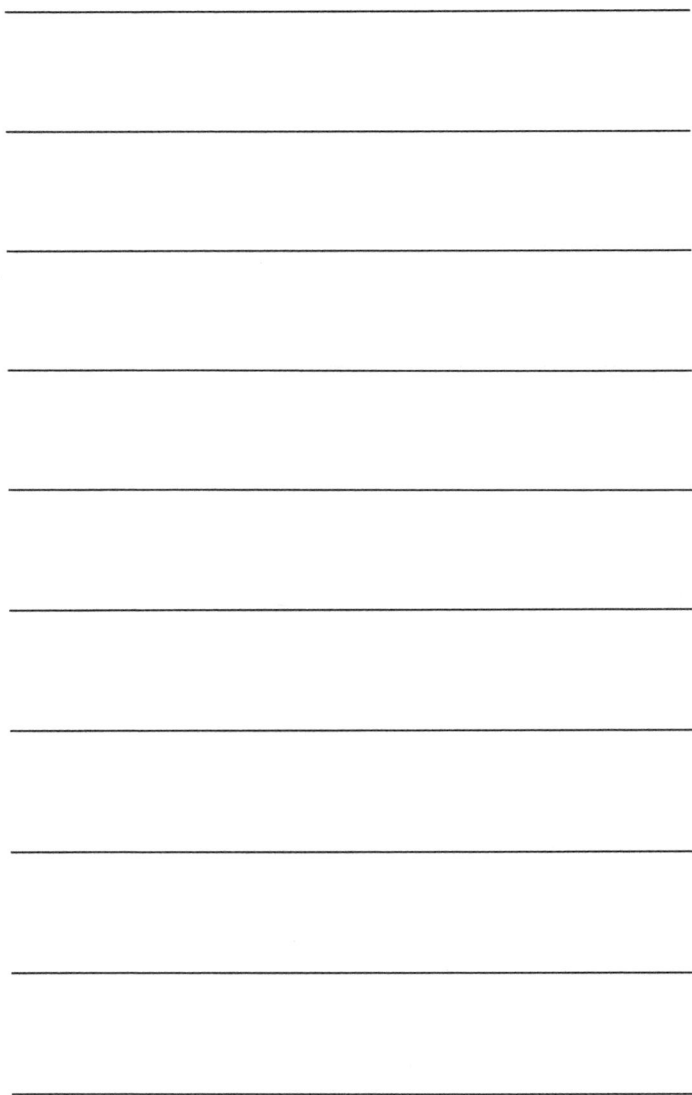

(3) What have you applied so far?

_____

_____

_____

_____

_____

_____

_____

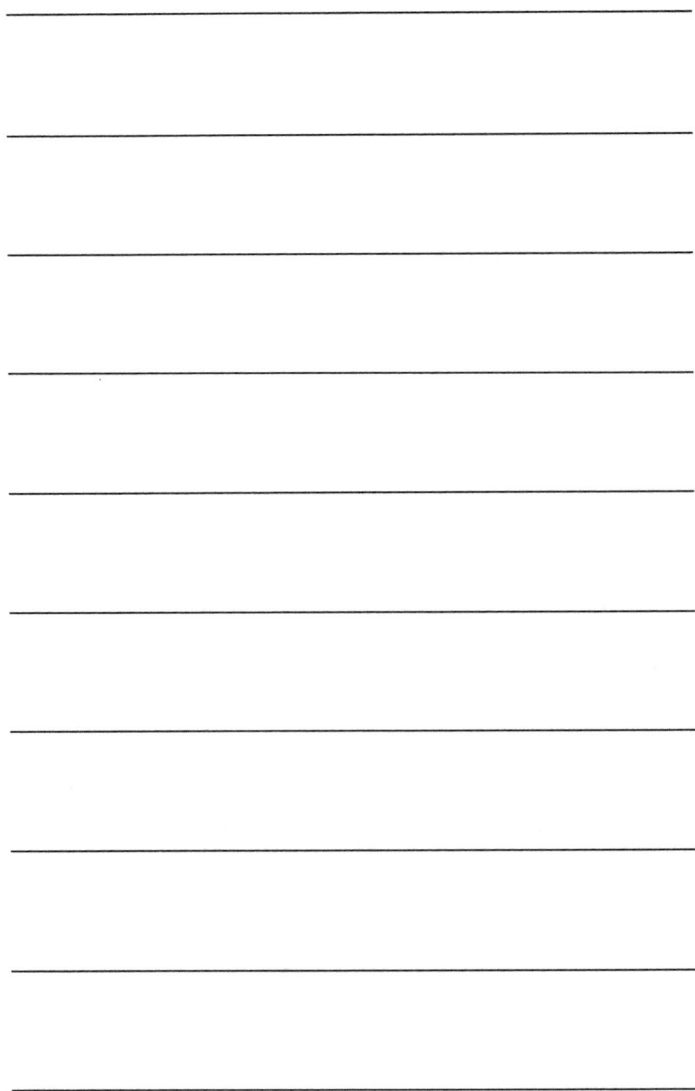

ABOUT THE AUTHORS

Bernice Harris is a long-time resident of the Chicago Englewood community, which has one of the highest crime rates in the city. Harris is very aware of the daily dangers that exist in that neighborhood, as well as other neighborhoods in the inner city. She has worked with teen runaways as well as with deaf youths through the Chicago Hearing Society. She has taught early childhood education in a corporate school owned by the former Secretary of Education, Lamar Alexander, and Bob Keeshan, better known as Captain Kangaroo.

Stefanie Newell has earned a stellar reputation as the go-to writing coach for the first time writer who's looking for direction on how to write and publish their first book. Through her writing, publishing, and marketing expertise, she helps aspiring writers to unleash their authentic voice and share their message through the pages of their book. Not only has she assisted beginners in bringing their book idea to fruition, but her expertise has also paved the way for her to coach an accomplished Hollywood film and television producer.

In addition to coaching authors through her **How To Write A Book program**, Stefanie is also an author of numerous fiction and non-fiction books.

More Titles From Write One Publications, Inc.

Non-fiction Titles

How To Write Your First Book

Write A Book Now!

Pull Your Pants Up and Be A Man!

Fiction Titles

Love, Fame, and Betrayal

Rules of The Game

www.ingramcontent.com/pod-product-compliance
Lightning Source LLC
Chambersburg PA
CBHW071453070426
42452CB00039B/1195